The U.S Marshal's Bride

Remy Marie

Copyright

Table of Contents

Prologue

"Are you ready? What's taking so long? I wanted to leave an hour ago." Henry McToole roared towards his wife, Abigail. His Irish accent was thick and impatient.

"I'm sorry Henry. I had to feed Thomas." Like her husband, Abigail had a thick Irish accent as well.

Henry rolled his eyes. "You could've done that while we rode."

"The ride is too bumpy for him to feed!" Abigail snapped

"Don't you dare raise your voice at me!" Henry growled as he glared at his wife. "It's bad enough I'm stuck on this ride with you. I don't be needin any lip ought you too."

Abigail cowered at his tone. "I'm sorry, Henry."

Henry stared at his wife before shaking his head and looking towards the horizon. "Pathetic, I'm starting to regret saying yes to your father's arrangement. You've been more a pain in my ass than what you're worth. You're lucky I'd made a promise to God to honor you. That vow is the only thing keeping us together. I promise to provide for you, but if you keep giving me lip, so help me…"

Abigail began to cry as she felt pain from her loveless marriage. She wasn't even sure how her marriage was started. One moment she met Henry, the next she found herself married and on a ship to a new land in America. As a little girl she dreamed of love and an honorable man, instead she got stuck with a drunk and a dreamer. At least she had Thomas. He was her one bright spot in the world of darkness.

"I'm sorry…" she muttered.

Henry spat tobacco and wiped his mouth with his sleeve.

"I bet you are…" his stare was cold and menacing. He shook his head and growled, "I don't even know why I waste my time with you." He grabbed a near by flask and took a sip before placing it back in his pocket. "The sooner we get to California, the sooner I get off this bloody carriage and away from you. Let's get a move on. Ha!" Henry yelled, snapping the reins to the horses.

They neighed and started to trot through the flat plain of the territories. Sitting next to her husband, Abigail looked at the vast wilderness of Kansas. There wasn't a spot of civilization in sight. As she rode, she was bucked back and forth from the rough terrain. The wood felt hard on her rear as she shifted back and forth. As she observed her surroundings, she noticed the morning sun that was stretching out on the prairie making it a wonderful sight, which was much better than her company.

Kansas was different from the streets of New York City. The land was wild and untamed. Instead of civilized men you found hostiles. Stray dogs became coyotes and stray cats became rattle snakes. Everything she saw wanted to kill her, yet the land around her was like a scenic painting.

Despite the magnificent view, she didn't choose this journey, her husband did. When her and her husband came to this country from Ireland, they heard tales about America and its fortunes west. Wanting a slice of his own, he sold everything they had, purchased a wagon, and started on the trail west.

It's been the tough journey between them. They've encountered more dangers than they cared to count, but each time they made it out unscathed. A sane person would have turned back months ago, but Henry had a goal and wanted to complete it at all costs.

Abigail was different. She didn't care for traveling. She just wanted a family and a good man to treat her right. She didn't care if she was New York, California, or even Kansas. She reckoned that home was where you decided it to be.

The couple rode in silence each looking the opposite direction. The trail didn't help their marriage. Instead, it tested it. They were already on rocky ground to begin with, and after Thomas was born, Abigail thought this would've been the adhesive to keep them together, but the passion between them sizzled out a long time ago.

Neither were paying attention as a stranger rode up to them.

"Good morning," The traveler grinned.

Abigail smiled at the man and noticed the long scar on his face.

"Hello," Henry replied.

"Where are you two headin'?"

"We're headin' to California."

"Just yourselves? No caravan?" He asked, searching around.

"No, just ourselves."

The man nodded. "It's dangerous to be traveling alone."

"We're aware, but we've made it this far." Henry replied.

"Oh, well, it's best not to count your chickens until they hatch." The man grabbed his pistol and aim it at Henry.

"How bout you stop the wagon and you and I talk?"

Henry looked at Abigail and then looked back at the outlaw.

"Please sir. All that we have is in the back of this wagon."

"You should have thought of that before you passed the Mississippi." The man pulled the hammer to the gun and growled, "I won't ask again. Stop the wagon."

Henry looked at Abigail before he attempted to reach to his side for his gun, but the bandit was faster as he shot Henry in the chest.

"Henry!" Abigail yelped.

Henry slumped back, gurgling blood. Abigail quickly grabbed the reins and snapped them, making the horses go faster. The outlaw followed her and she could hear the horse's hooves clap the dirt as he gained distance. Her heart was beating out of her chest and tears ran down her cheeks as she prayed that she'd make it alive with her son.

Across the horizon she saw a gang of men galloping towards her. She smiled as they raced towards her.

"I'm saved." She waved her arms. "Help me! Help me!" She begged.

As she approached them, they'd stopped in a straight line with the guns pointed towards her.

When Abigail got closer to them, she slowed her wagon and pointed behind her.

"That man, he's killed my husband. Please you have to help."

"Sorry ma'am. We ain't the calvary, we're the robbers."

Abigail sat there in shock and the only thing running though her brain was Thomas. She knew she had to protect him.

"Please sir, don't kill me. It's just my son and me now. Please don't."

The man with the scar rode up to her and stood in front of the gang of men.

"I won't shoot ya, but that was my warning to you when I killed your husband. Leave the wagon, and I'll spare you and your son."

"Please…"

The man with the scar pointed the gun at her and Abigail screamed in fear.

"Leave the wagon or I will shoot. Final warning." He pulled back the hammer and Abigail closed her eyes.

"Okay! I'll do it. Just let me get my son. He's in the back."

"Okay, go on and no funny business or I'll shoot you in the back."

Abigail nodded and rose her hands as she walked towards the back of her wagon. Thomas was laying in a bed of blankets and Abigail swaddled him, before crawling back out.

"Okay, I have him."

"Pleasure doing business with you, ma'am. Men, let's ride."

One of the goons hopped off his horse and onto the wagon. The group of men rode away leaving Abigail in a dust cloud of hopelessness. As the sun beamed down on her, she fell to her knees crying. Sobbing she clutched Thomas tighter, wondering how she could get out of this predicament.

Chapter 1

Sam rode his horse down the road tilting his cap at every man and woman he saw. As he said good morning, most of the travelers didn't pay him any mind. Some stared, others held their heads up to him.

Sam was used to it as he was a black man of the law. Those people were more in shock than anything. His golden US Marshal badge shined in the limited light from the sunset and his black trench coat, pants, vest, and white shirt were flawlessly cleaned and unripped. His black leather boots weren't worn down or second hand. Everything he wore, was first class, which wasn't a class often reserved for a black man.

He knew that black men in power seemed to throw people off. However, it made sense as it was only five years ago that he escaped from his former masters and joined up with the Union army to fight the confederates. It was only five years ago that white people had all the power in the world. It was only right that it didn't set well with folks that he had power over them.

The sun was settling in the trading post town known as Samson. The flat prairie town was often used as a stopping point for folks on the trail west, with more travelers than actual locals. Down the main road there were several homes and business, including a hotel, saloon, general store, clothing boutique, and parlor. Outside the main road there wasn't many homes. There was some temporary tents and wagons, put up by travelers, but the town didn't have many other citizens that lived there.

The town was so small that they didn't have a mayor or a local lawman. The people there governed themselves. Sam was the closest thing to a sheriff in town as he was posted there looking for things like cattle thieves and bandits looking to score on innocent travelers. He watched out for the locals, and they watched out for his home that he had in town.

As he rode down the road, he came upon a young woman and her infant. She looked to be begging for help, but no one would stop to help her. Her brunette hair was braided, but in disarray and she had a slim figure. Dirt covered her face, and her dress was torn in several areas. Sam guessed that she probably hadn't eaten much in days. The baby was crying loudly as people passed by.

Sam never seen them before as he recognized most people in town, but wasn't surprised that they looked unfamiliar as their outpost was in the middle of nowhere and had many wagons that pass through it. It was a sad sight to see as no one helped her. He had no idea how long she'd been out there begging as he just arrived in town after catching a pair of outlaws wanted by the law.

Upon seeing her, Sam rode up to her and tipped his cap.

"Ma'am, is there a problem?"

"Yes, she cried. "Please help me. I am desperate. I am with child, and bandits killed my husband and stole everything I had. We need food and shelter, but no one wants to give it."

"I can." Sam replied.

"Oh, thank you."

Sam nodded and hopped off his horse.

"May I?" He asked, pointing towards her waist.

She nodded and Sam grabbed her hips and lifted her onto her horse.

"How bout you stay off your feet til we get back to my home."

"Thank you. That's mighty kind of you."

Sam tilted his cap again and led her down the road.

"So, tell me miss, do you have a name?"

"Abigail McToole."

"Nice to meet you, Abigail. My name is Sam Wilson. What brought you to town?"

"My husband and I were going west. He was killed by some outlaws. I ran into some cowboys who took me to the nearest town, which is here."

"I'm sorry to hear about your husband, ma'am."

"Thank you, Sam." Abigail stared at Sam and then replied, "it's not often you see a colored lawman."

Sam laughed. "No, I'm a rare breed. I got this badge from my services in the war. If anyone has a problem with it, they can talk to my steel." Sam patted his gun on his hip and Abigail smiled.

"You seem like you're a good man."

"I am, right this way ma'am." Sam grinned as he led her to a one room shack at the end of the road.

"Is this your house?"

"Yes, it ain't much, but it keeps my hat dry."

"No, it's lovely."

"Thank you, ma'am. Come on inside. I got some beans and jerky that I could feed you."

"Thank you."

Walking in, Abigail looked around the room, which included a bed, a small stove in the corner and a table with one chair. On the opposite side was a small tub. The most unusual item in the house was a small piano.

She smiled at the instrument and asked, "do you play?"

Sam looked at the piano and chuckled, "not in a long time. My hands are usually used to serve justice these days."

"Oh…" Abigail observed the room and noticed that there was a lot of dust settled in the house and it looked like the Marshal rarely stayed in the room. In addition, judging by the small dining table with one chair and bed, she assumed that he was alone.

"Is it just you here? Do you have a wife?" Abigail asked.

Sam smirked. "No wife, it's just me. Here, come take a seat. I'll get you fixed with somethin' to eat."

Sam grabbed some beans, jerky and a day old biscuit and placed it on a tin plate. He also poured a glass of water and brought it towards Abigail.

"Here you go, miss." He replied, placing it on the table.

"Thank you, Sam."

He tipped his hat again and then walked around the room grabbing a wooden crate and a pillow.

"What's that for?" She asked.

"While I don't have a crib, I could make one for you if you want, but in the meantime, here's a bed for the little one."

"Aww that's kind of you. You're more decent than most men I've met. Everyone in town just went about their day, they didn't even ask if they could help. You're the first man who did."

"I'm just doing what any decent man should." He replied. "May I?" He pointed to her baby.

Abigail hesitated.

"It's okay. I'm just going to place it in the crib so that you can eat with both hands. I promise, I'll be careful. I was the oldest in my family, so I grew up taking care of my mama's babies. I know how to hold them."

Abigail nodded and handed him her child.

Sam cradled the baby's head and shushed him as he rocked him back and forth.

"What's his name?"

"Thomas," Abigail replied as she took a bite of her food.

"Hi, Thomas." Sam grinned while making kissing noises. Thomas' small hand touched Sam's cheek and smiled.

"He likes you." Abigail smirked.

"Nah, he's probably ain't used to seeing a negro man." Sam kept, rocking Thomas until he fell asleep and then placed him in the makeshift crib.

"That was impressive. He's been cranky most of the day. You weren't lying about being good with kids.

"Aww, he was probably tired from the day." Sam walked towards his pantry and gathered some food for himself on a plate. He ate half the plate before looking back at Abigail.

"So, where you heading?"

"California. My deceased husband and I are from Ireland, and we immigrated to New York looking for a better life. My husband heard about more opportunities in California, so we hitched a wagon and went on the trail."

"You couldn't afford to take the train?"

"No, sir. Tickets were too expensive. Personally, I would have rather stayed in New York, but my husband insisted we go. He always was a dreamer."

"I'm sorry to hear about your late husband."

"It's okay. While my husband and I had our differences, he didn't deserve to be shot like he did."

Sam nodded. "Do you know where'd you be goin next?"

"No, honestly, I had hoped to figure it out at California, but now I'm not so sure. Is there work available in town?"

"I'm not sure. I can ask around."

"What about the parlor?"

Sam shook his head, "that place is no place for a mother. They won't care for you or Thomas. You'll stay with me until you can get your feet under you."

"Stay with you?"

"Yes, is that a problem?"

"No, but how can I repay you? I have no money."

"It's a'ight Abigail. No payment needed. You and the little one is free to stay."

Abigail bit her lip looking away and then looked back at Sam. "It doesn't feel right to take your kindness without giving something back. You are unmarried, are you not?"

"I am..." Sam replied, wondering where Abigail was going with her question.

"Then allow me to marry you."

"Abigail..." Sam began to say before she cut him off.

"I will be a good woman to you. I can cook, clean and make love with you if you so desire."

"I don't desire any of those things."

Abigail scrunched up her face.

"What? Do you not find me attractive?"

"Near the opposite. I find you to be the prettiest woman I've seen. Your brown eyes are like nothing I've ever seen before. Just looking at you now feels like I'm having a heart attack. When I first saw you, I was surprised that someone would ignore a beautiful woman such as yourself."

"If that is so, why won't you take me as yours? I am a widow. I belong to no one."

"Is your heart not with your late husband?"

"No, he and I were arranged by our parents. A deal was stuck, and before I knew it, I was whisked away to America and promised a great many things that were never delivered to me."

"Oh, I am sorry to hear."

"That's in the past now. I am offering to be yours. Would you take it?"

Sam hesitated and then shook his head. "No, I won't."

Abigail's jaw dropped. "So, I am to leave then?"

"No, not at all. This house is yours and Thomas, until you can find your own."

"Why give me shelter but not marry me?"

Sam shrugged. "I do not wish to marry out of necessity. My heart will go to a woman who will love me, and their heart will be mine as well."

Abigail nodded, "that's sweet of you. I can learn to love you."

Sam shook his head. "To love a negro man is more than expressing words. Our coupling would be frowned upon by many. The townsfolk here might accept it, but any visitors that comes through would treat you like trash. A white woman and a negro man is considered an abomination in this country. We may be free, but we're still slaves to the white man's rules."

Abigail sighed. "I not saying that I've been through the same life experiences as you had Sam, but I do know what it's like to be treated like trash. As an immigrant, I was too often looked down upon. I'm sorry that I didn't fully understand the struggle."

"It's quite a'ight, Abigail."

"At least let me repay you in some way."

"Your smile is all the payment I need." Sam grinned.

Abigail blushed as she looked down at her shoes. She then looked back up at Sam with a wide smile. "That's mighty kind of you."

Sam nodded and then finished his plate. "Now, it looks like you've been through hell and back. How bout a bath? I can go and fetch some hot water for you."

"Aww, Sam, that would be wonderful."

"Great, I'll be right back. You go ahead and get settled."

Abigail nodded and finished her meal. She helped clean Sam's plate and then washed them in a sink nearby. After drying them, she went to check on Thomas who was snoring comfortably. She brushed his brown hair and then leaned forward to kiss her forehead.

"He seems like a good man." She whispered to her baby. "He's at least more honorable than your father.

Sleep well little Prince." She kissed him once more before, sitting back up. She explored his room further looking at the wall of collectibles that he had, including a Union soldier's uniform, a saber and a photograph that looked to be a picture with a bunch of black soldiers. Abigail stared at the picture and found a younger Sam, standing in the far left.

Abigail smiled at the picture and then moved to sit on the bed. The bed was firm, but it was more comfortable than sleeping on the ground like she's been doing for the last couple of weeks. This was the first night she wasn't moving or worried about animals or bandits attacking her at night. It was nice just to relax.

Sam entered the room with a large metal basin filled with water. The steam was rising from the barrel as he carried it with ease. Abigail was impressed at his strength as he shuffled his feet across the room. Not one drop was spilled as he filled up the tub.

"I'll be right back for the second load." He replied, walking out.

"Thank you." Abigail replied.

He nodded and walked back out the house.

Abigail touched the warm water and was excited as she couldn't remember the last time she had a warm bath. Abigail began to untie her dress and was in her white shift when Sam entered the room again.

"Oh, pardon me ma'am. I didn't realize that you'd be getting undress at this moment."

"It's quite alright, Sam. Do you like what you see?"

Sam's eyes lingered on Abigail's body and a stray chill ran up his spine. For once in his life, he was speechless as he stared at her slim figure.

"Hmm...what about now?" Abigail pushed the straps of her chemise off and stood naked in front of him. Sam felt his trousers get tight as he ballooned in size. His eyes couldn't stop staring at her perky breasts and her smooth pale thighs.

"Abigail..."

"Yes?"

"You are a diamond along rocks. God took his time with your beauty, I can admit that much."

Abigail blushed again. She pushed a strand of her brown hair back behind her ear. "If you like what you see, why won't you lay with me?"

"I told you, Abigail...you may be physically gifted, but my heart still must decide as should yours. I value the bond of marriage and it shouldn't be decided based on need, but of that of love."

Abigail grinned at his admission as it gave her butterflies. "You truly are an honorable man."

"I try to be." He winked as he dumped the second barrel of water into the tub. "Now, that should do it. Go ahead and step in."

Abigail nodded and groaned as she felt the warm wet touch her skin.

"Too hot?" Sam asked.

"Just right," She grinned as she sunk her body into the water.

"Perfect. I'll go and fetch the soap. Stay right there."

Abigail sat in the tub and watch Sam walk around the room collecting various items. Sitting there it was the first time she was catered to by a man. Normally it was her mother or herself getting things, but this was the opposite. Sam grabbed soap, a towel and found a large clean tunic for her to wear to bed.

Once she was clean, Sam opened a towel for her and then wrapped the towel around her. Abigail dried herself off, and then dropped the towel, to grab the tunic.

Sam looked away as she got dressed.

Abigail laughed and shook her head. "I think we are a bit past looking away, don't you think?"

Sam laughed, "I do, but we aren't married, and you are still a lady. You shall be treated with respect while you dress."

"That's sweet of you. A'ight, I'm done."

Sam looked back at Abigail and laughed as the tunic reached her knees.

"That's really big on you."

"It is, but it's a great nightgown. Thank you for everything, Sam."

"You're welcome. Get some rest you deserve it."

"Thank you, Sam." Abigail climbed into bed and then rose her eyebrows when she saw Sam leaving the house. "And where do you think you're going?"

"Theres a nice rocker on the porch calling my name."

"You're not sleeping in the bed?"

"No, ma'am. It's okay, I've slept in worse places, and that rocker has put me to sleep more times than I care to admit."

"I will not force a man out of his own bed. Please I insist."

"Abigail, we're not married..."

"I understand, but I also want the man who'd cared for me to be comfortable. Please. Do it for me."

Sam hesitated and then sighed. He removed his shoes, gun belt, vest and jacket and then climbed into bed with Abigail. As he got comfortable, Abigail placed her arm across his chest.

"Is this too much?"

"No, ma'am. That's a'ight with me."

"Good. Night Sam." Abigail kissed his cheek and then snuggled against him.

"Goodnight," Sam whispered as he held her hand. He stared at her, before his eyes got heavy and he drifted off to sleep.

Chapter 2

Abigail woke up to the sounds of wood being chopped. She stretched in the bed and looked around her surroundings. Last night seemed to feel like a dream. Between the food, the bath, the bed, and the company, she'd never been treated to such hospitality since she'd arrived to the country. Sam was a godsend as she didn't know how much longer she could have survived without him.

Sitting up in bed, she looked to her left and found that Thomas was sleeping soundly in the crate. She rolled out of bed and kissed him before walking towards the window to find the origin of the noise that woke her up.

To her delight she found a sweaty shirtless Sam splitting logs in two with an ax. He was wearing only his pants, with the straps of his suspenders down to his hips. His dark skin glistened in the sun as beads of sweat rolled off his muscular body.

She'd seen men chop wood before, but something about the way Sam did it stirred her loins like never before. Her breathing became shallowed, and her heart quivered. She took a step closer to the window and placed one hand on the glass, while the other rested on her rapidly beating chest.

She wasn't sure what was coming over her. She felt lightheaded, watching the man work. She ogled his stature, and her eyes trailed down to the bulge between his legs. Upon seeing it her thighs became wet and her mind wondered what if.

When Sam finished chopping wood, he wiped his brow and picked up the split pieces carrying them to the house.

When Abigail saw him approach, she panicked and didn't know what to to as she didn't want him to know she was gawking at him. Quickly she jumped back onto the bed just as the door was opening.

"Oh, you're awake." Sam grinned. "Sleep well?"

"I did. How about yourself?"

"Yes, it was interesting sharing a bed."

"I rather enjoyed it."

"So did I." The two stared at each other smiling before Sam cleared his throat. "Well, I brought some wood for the stove in case you need to use it. I also placed five dollars on the table there. Feel free to use it for food or any other provisions that you may need."

"Thank you, Sam. Once again, your kindness is beyond words."

He grinned and began placing the stack of sticks by the stove.

"And where would you go?" Abigail asked.

"I have business at a ranch nearby. The rancher told me that there's been some suspicious characters lingering nearby and I'm riding out to talk to them." Sam dusted off his hands and then found his shirt. He buttoned it and then placed his vest over it.

"Oh, do you think it would be dangerous?"

"I don't think so, but if it is, I can handle it." Sam placed on his coat and made sure that his U.S Marshal badge was visible. Grabbing his gun belt, he tied his two guns to his hips.

"Oh, I still don't like the sound of that."

Sam walked closer to Abigail and touched her cheek. Abigail shivered from his touch.

"I promise. I'll be safe. You have my word." He reassured, putting on his hat.

Abigail smiled and nodded. "Okay."

Sam's hand slipped down to her chin and lifted her head up to meet his eyes.

"Goddamn, you got some beautiful eyes. I promise. I'll see you tonight."

The two lingered and Abigail's mouth watered as she thought she was going to receive a kiss from him, but instead Sam walked away, heading outside.

"Goodbye Abigail. Have a good day."

"You too," Abigail replied, watching him leave to get on his horse. With a loud, "ha!" He kicked his horse, and he was gone.

Abigail stood there wondering the feeling that she felt. His touch gave her goosebumps and the way he stared at her felt like he was peering into her soul. Her thoughts about him drifted until she was awakened from them by Thomas.

"Oh, Thomas. Shh...Shh..." she comforted as she picked him up. "I know you are hungry. Momma's got you. Momma's here." She pushed the tunic down allowing Thomas to feed. As he did, Abigail couldn't stop thinking of Sam. She didn't know what this feeling was, but she liked it.

After feeding her child, she changed his diaper and got dressed herself. She hated that she had to wear the same tattered clothes, but they were all that she had.

She found a small ball in Sam's room and gave it to Thomas to play with as she cleaned up his house. While she knew that she wasn't his wife, it was the least she could do considering he took her in. She dusted, swept, washed out his sink and tub, cleaned out the stove, and did his laundry. By the time she was done it was midday. She wiped her brow and grabbed lunch enjoying some leftover beans and jerky, and allowed Thomas to feed once more.

When she was done, she got dressed and took Thomas out to head to the general store. As she walked, she noticed that many people would stare at her. Some whispered and others giggled. She wasn't sure what they were laughing or talking about, but she paid them no mind. She held on to Thomas more tightly though.

As she pushed the door to the general store, a bell dinged and the shopkeeper grumbled, "I'll be with you in a minute."

"Okay, thank you," Abigail replied, browsing through his wares. The general store was small with only three rows of goods. It included all a man or woman would need for a life in the prairie, including, food, clothes, equipment and guns. Abigail always liked stores like these. It made it easier for her to shop and not go to four or five different stores.

"What can I do ya for?"

"Yes, I was curious if you had any fresh sausages."

"Yeah, butcher came through here with some. Let me check the ice box."

"I also want to see if you have any potatoes and beans?"

"Yep, just give me a minute." He replied, collecting the materials.

He wrapped the sausage in parchment and placed it in a basket along with the potatoes and a can of beans.

"Be needin anything else ma'am?"

"No, that should do it."

He nodded. "Three dollars."

Abigail handed him the cash, and he placed it in the register.

"Thank you," Abigail replied, walking out.

"Ma'am wait, weren't you that woman who was standing outside of town begging?"

"I was."

"Where did ya get the money to pay for this?

"From Sam Wilson."

"The negro?" The shopkeeper chuckled. "Are you staying with him?"

"I am...is there a problem with that?"

"No, problem from me ma'am. Sam's a good man, but you might want to watch out for some travelers around here. Some of them don't take to kind to a white woman sleeping with a negro man."

"We're not doing anything illegal."

"Some people might think you are. Just be careful is all I'm saying. Have a good day."

"Thank you, sir. You as well." Abigail left the store and carried her son in one hand, while carrying the basket in the other. As she walked down the street, she heard more whispers and laughs. Before she didn't know what they were talking about, but now she knew. She knew that they were laughing at her.

She ignored their quips and their monkey calls. She didn't let their harassment bother her. She kept her head held high as she suffered from the men and women's abuse. Eventually a man moved in her way and scratched his arms and made sounds like a monkey.

"Are you attracted to this?" He laughed.

"Go to hell!" Abigail spat.

"Funny you should say that. That's exactly where you'll end up for laying with that negro man." The man laughed. "Why is that? Hmm, is it because you can't find a decent white man to fuck? Don't worry baby, I can be that man for you…" the stranger reached out and touched Abigail's cheek.

"Don't you dare touch me!" She yelled, kicking him.

"Why I oughta!" He reached for his gun but before he could pull the pistol, Sam rode up and aimed his gun at the man's chest.

"Do it. I dare you. Go ahead and pull that gun and you'd be dead before you could fire a shot."

"I'm just messing with her Marshal." He replied, noticing the badge on his coat jacket.

"From the way I see it, you were assaulting her."

"I wasn't, I swear."

"My eyes tell me otherwise. You listen here and you listen well. I may be a negro, but my badge says differently. My badge tells you that I am the law. I am the judge, jury and executioner in these parts. I can shoot you dead and there's not a damn thing anyone could do about it."

"Please…" he begged.

"Leave this town. I don't care where you go, but if I ever see your face again. It would be your last. You understand?"

"Yes, sir." The man ran to his horse and rode off. As he left Sam looked at everyone around him.

"That warning goes to all of you. Miss McToole is an extension of me. You mess with her. You mess with me. Think long and hard before you make any comments about her. Understood?"

The crowd muttered and went about their business. As they dispersed Sam looked back at Abigail.

"Are you okay?"

"I'm fine. I've dealt with assholes before. I know how to handle them."

"I see that." Sam chuckled. "I was wrong about you."

"In what way?"

"You are a capable woman who's not afraid of the devil himself."

Abigail grinned. "When it comes to people I care about, I can become a wolf with fangs."

"That I see. It's kind of you to care for me."

"Sam, I care for you more than you know."

Sam and Abigail smiled at each other before, Sam hopped off his horse and offered it to Abigail to ride. Once more he helped her up and once more, he felt the electricity surge between them.

"Did you pick up anything good?" Sam asked, looking at the basket.

"I did. I planned on cooking your dinner before I got interrupted."

"Please don't let me stop you on my account. I'm famished."

"Good, come on." Abigail grinned, leading him back to his house.

Walking in, Sam whistled looking at the cleaned home.

"When I took you in, I didn't expect this. Wow, Abigail this place is spotless."

"Thank you, Sam. It's the least I could do." Abigail placed Thomas in the crate and then took the food towards the stove to prepare the dinner. As she did, Sam helped to get the stove hot, and then sat at the dinner table watching her prepare the food. He couldn't help but to smile staring at her hips as she cooked. His mind drifted towards last night when he saw her naked and like before his cock swelled from the sensual image. He tried to control it, but there was no denying the fact that he was becoming smitten by her.

"You know I was impressed how you handled that asshole in town today. I was worried how the world would see us together, but you seemed unfazed by what people said or did."

"That's because I'm Irish. I was born with tough skin."

Sam laughed. "Thanks for the reminder. I guess I shouldn't get on your bad side."

"No, you shouldn't." She winked.

Sam could hear the sausages sizzle as she cooked them in the skillet.

"Smells good. What are you making?"

"Bangers and Mash. A great hearty meal."

"Sounds lovely."

Abigail smiled back at him.

Watching her cook, Sam admired her from afar and wondered about how her late husband lucked out on such a jewel.

"Tell me, did you love your late husband?"

Abigail hesitated and bit her lip. "Love is such a strong word. Perhaps at one time there was passion, but it was long extinguished."

"I'm sorry to hear. I can't imagine falling out of love with a woman such as yourself. Beauty and you take care of a household. You are a wonder."

Abigail felt the warmth in her cheeks yet again as she found herself breathless. She wondered how it was possible for a man to make her feel such a way. She couldn't explain it but every second she spent with him she found herself wanting him like no man she'd ever wanted before. When she was with him time seemed to sit still.

"Supper is ready." She grinned as she placed all the components on a tin plate.

"Thank you, Abigail. It smells delicious."

"Thank you," she replied, placing the food in front of him. She then fixed herself a plate and brought over a wooden crate to sit on next to Sam.

"Mmm, Abigail, if you cook like this, I'm going to have to keep you myself."

Abigail laughed. "You might be careful, because to me that sounds like a marriage proposal."

Sam chuckled. "How many people do you reckon get married after tasting a meal?"

"We will surely be the first."

"Ha, I can see it now when folks asks us why we got hitched and I'll tell them that one bite from your food made me fall in love with you."

Abigail giggled. "Well, if I would have known that cooking for you would have swept you off your feet, I would have done it last night."

"I should have requested it." Sam finished the last piece of sausage by sliding it through the mash potatoes and bean gravy. He took the final bite and groaned.

"Care for some more?" She asked.

"Yes, please."

Abigail smiled and grabbed his plate. She went back to the stove to get a second helping and then returned with another plate of food.

"Thank you, Abigail."

"My pleasure," she resumed eating and then looked over at the piano on the wall. "When was the last time you played?" She asked, pointing to it.

"It's been a while. Would you like me to play you a tune?"

"I would love it."

Sam grinned and finished his meal. After wiping his face with a napkin, he walked over to the piano, and flexed his fingers.

"Any requests?"

"Play whatever you feel."

Sam nodded and cleared his throat. He played a soft tune and began singing about a man and woman falling in love. Listening to his beautiful voice, Abigail sat there in a daze. Once more she felt butterflies in her stomach. Sam had a voice of an angel. His serenade was magical, and it put her under a spell. She couldn't explain her next moves as she stood up and placed her hands on his shoulders.

Sam leaned back, embracing her touch. His body trembled as he smelled her feminine musk. He could feel her cheek on his head as she held him close.

"Sam?" Abigail whispered.

"Yes?"

"Care to dance with me?"

"I would love to." He replied.

He stood up, turned around, and pulled Abigail close to him. The couple dance slowly, looking into each other's eyes. Both of them felt the same emotion as their passions grew for each other every second. Their breathing increased steadily as the romantic tension in the air grew.

"Sam…I…"

"Shh, don't speak," he begged placing a finger on her mouth.

Abigail shivered from his touch. Inch by inch the two drew closer. Abigail licked her lips and puckered her mouth preparing for the kiss that came, however instead of a kiss she heard Thomas cry.

Sam pulled away and cleared his throat as if he was awakened from a dream.

"It sounds like Thomas needs you." Sam whispered.

"Yes, I uhh…" Abigail was at a lost of words as she hesitated in her next moves. "Yes, I will see to him." She finally stuttered. She walked away from Sam towards Thomas and picked him out of the crate. She cradled him in her arms and rocked him back and forth.

"He's probably just hungry. Give me a moment."

"Take as much time as you need." Sam replied.

Abigail nodded and sat on the bed with Thomas. Sam returned back to the table to clean up the dishes from their supper. As he did, he caught a peek of Abigail breast feeding Thomas. Realizing that she was exposed, Sam quickly looked away and resumed cleaning. However, the nurturing image he saw still remained in his brain. He thought about what a family would be like with her. He wondered what would their children look like. He's seen mulatto children before, and each one he's seen was always different. Some looked more white others looked more black. He was curious on where a child with Abigail would fit in this world.

He worried that the child would experience extreme prejudice like he did, but the more he thought about it, the more he realized that regardless of who he had a child with, they were going to face racism. He was black and they would be black too.

He knew that they won't get love from the outside world. Instead, they would have to receive love from the father and mother, and upon watching Abigail interact with Thomas he knew that she would love her child no matter what their skin color was.

After washing the dishes, Sam sat back down and watched as Abigail placed a sleeping Thomas back into his crate.

"He's fine now."

"Did you want to keep dancing?" She asked.

"I'm actually tired. Did you want to go to bed?"

Abigail smiled and nodded her head. "I would love too."

Abigail removed her shoes and her dress, to be in her white shift. While Sam removed his coat, vest, and boots. He removed the straps of his suspenders and allowed them to drape at his hips as he climbed into bed with Abigail. The two cuddled close as they held each other. Abigail held his hand and made circular motions with her thumb. As she did, Sam looked at her, and then Thomas who was snoozing quietly. He then looked at her tattered dress and frowned.

"Abigail?" He whispered.

Abigail turned in the bed to face him. "Yes?"

"How would you like me to take you dress shopping tomorrow."

"Are you sure you could afford that? I don't want to be a burden to your finances."

Sam reached out and rubbed her cheek. "You and Thomas are the furthest thing from a burden to me. I care you for and you can't be walking around in a tattered dress. Please, let me help."

Abigail smiled and nodded. "Thank you,"

Sam pushed back a strand of her hair and whispered, "you're welcome. Good night, Abigail."

"Good night, Sam," she grinned before turning back around and allowing Sam to cuddle close to her.

Chapter 3

It's been a while since Abigail went dress shopping. The last time she brought a dress was in New York right before they left to head west. Walking down the street, Abigail walked beside Sam to a nearby boutique. In her hand was Thomas, who was watching all the commotion on Main Street with great interest. As the couple walked close many people eyeballed them whispering and pointing at Sam and Abigail.

Sam noticed the stares and leaned closer to Abigail to whisper, "are you sure your okay with us walking together?"

"Yes, I told you. I don't care about their stares or their gossip. As an immigrant, I'm used to the disapproving looks. It is nothing new to me, I have thick skin remember?"

"Aw, yes. I remember. Tough as leather I recall."

"Yes. We Irish are just built differently."

Sam chuckled. "Of course."

"Well, if they are going to stare, we might as well give them a show. Come closer to me."

Sam stood nearby Abigail, and she hooked her arm through his to hold his hand. This seemed to ignite the crowd more as they received more disapproving stares and whispers.

"Oh, you certainly stirred the pot."

"Good, let them watch as I'm currently holding the hand of the most honorable man in town. They'd only wish that you were there's."

Sam grinned, "is that so?"

Abigail winked at him, and they both laughed as they walked towards the dress boutique. Walking into the store, the bell rang, and a woman walked from the back room.

"Sam, welcome." She greeted. The woman had a strong French accent.

"Madame Eva, how are you today?"

"Much better now that I get to meet the talk of our town. Our own U.S Marshal Sam Wilson, with a woman. I thought you'd never get hitched."

Sam and Abigail looked at each other and laughed.

"Madame Eva, Abigail is just a guest in my home. Nothing more."

"Find that hard to believe. A beauty like her is hard to resist."

Sam felt his cheeks grow warm as he looked away.

"Aww you see, there's some magic in your eyes."

"Madame, we are not here to talk about us. We need a new dress."

"Yes, I see. These rags you are wearing are terrible. Come, let me get you set with something new."

"Thank you. Sam, do you mind watching Thomas?"

"No not at all," he grinned, taking the baby from her. Sam started to make baby noises and Thomas giggled at his voice. Abigail smiled and then followed Madame Eva to her sets of dresses.

The shopkeeper had a large assortment of dresses, most were dresses that would fit in the style of one living on a prairie. Abigail opted for a long brown skirt, along with a white shirt. After being fitted for the dress, the Madame made adjustments and took in the dress some to match Abigail's petite frame. Once she was done, Abigail got dressed in her new clothes and grinned as the fabric felt amazing.

Walking out of the dressing room, Abigail saw Sam and Thomas sitting in the corner of the shop. Sam was making funny faces at Thomas making him laugh. Abigail smiled at their interactions as they were both so cute. She cleared her throat causing Sam to look up.

The moment he saw her he gasped. His jaw nearly hit the floor as his words escaped him.

"Abigail..." he breathed.

"Do you like it?" She asked, twirling her dress.

"I think I might have died and gone to heaven. That dress on you..." he whistled as he continued to stare. "You are beautiful." He admitted.

"Thank you." She blushed.

Madame Eva stood at the corner of the shop watching the two interact.

Sam looked towards the shopkeeper and smiled. "Madame, I think you've out done yourself."

"Don't give me any compliments. Abigail radiates in that dress. She's the one that deserves all the praise."

"I guess you're right. How much do I owe you?"

"It's twenty dollars." Sam paid the shopkeeper the amount and then crooked his arm for Abigail to put her arm through. "Are you ready to leave Miss McToole?"

"Thank you, Mr. Wilson." She giggled, cuddling up close to him. The threesome left the shop and strolled down Main Street.

"Now that I have this dress, what now?" Abigail asked.

"I'm free to go where you want to go. We can head to the salon and get lunch, or we could go for a ride and have a picnic."

"Oh, a picnic..." Abigail halted her words and stood frozen as she looked away.

"Abigail what is it?" Sam questioned. He followed her eyes to a man with a large scar on his face.

"That man..." Abigail trembled.

"Do you know him?"

"He killed my husband."

"That man is outlaw Buster Briggs. He's wanted in at least three states. He has a lot of nerve showing here."

"What are you going to do?"

"Take Thomas and hide in my house until I get back."

"What are you going to do?"

"Take Thomas and go." Sam repeated.

"Sam please don't do this."

"This man attempted to hurt you. No one does that. Now get home. I'll see you soon."

Abigail hesitated and then nodded. She grabbed his hand and stared into his eyes.

"Come back to me."

"I will," he winked.

Abigail took Thomas and ran back to the house. Once she was in a safe distance, Sam walked towards Buster Briggs. His fingers flexed as he knew he would have to quick draw against him. Men like Buster only knew violence.

"Buster Briggs!" Sam called out. The outlaw turned around and smiled.

"And you are?"

"My name is Sam Wilson. US Marshal. By order of the court, you are found guilty of numerous crimes including robbery and murder. You have two options. Jail or death."

"I choose neither..." Buster reached for his gun, but Sam was faster as he shot the outlaw in the chest. He slumped to the floor and before Sam could check on him an explosion of gunfire occurred from several people, and Sam ran taking cover as he fired blindly striking two men.

The firefight was fierce as Sam was outnumbered four to one. Sam figured that this was the members of Buster's gang. The group traded blows, but Sam was the better shot, hitting three of them. When the last one stood, he retreated running towards his horse.

Sam left cover and aimed his gun at the man's back. Taking a deep breath, he shot the man long distance. Once the last man was down, Sam reloaded his gun and assessed the area. Most of the townsfolk had retreated into their homes and shops, but when the gunfire halted, they all walked out, looking at the dropped bodies.

"Sam, is it over?" The general store owner asked.

"Yes, it appears to be. It's safe now."

"You want some help with the bodies?"

"Yes, I'll spilt the bounty on these men for your help. Let's load them up in those caskets you got around back, until the judge can ride in town."

"Yes, sir." The shopkeeper replied as he grabbed the shoulders of the dead Buster Briggs and dragged him across the street. Sam did the same for another man he killed. Once the two were done, Sam looked back at the shopkeeper.

"Thank you for your help. I'm going back to my house to check on Abigail. If any trouble happens, let me know."

"Yes, sir," the shopkeeper replied.

Sam tipped his cap and then walked back to his house. When he opened the door, he found Abigail sitting in the bed crying and Thomas sleeping in his crate. The moment she saw him she stood up and slapped him.

Sam opened his eyes wide staring at her.

"Don't you ever do that again." Abigail cried.

"I can't promise you that."

"Why not?"

"Because you are my woman and as my woman, any man, creature or God himself threatens you, they will meet my wrath."

"I'm yours?"

"If you'd have me." Sam replied.

Abigail smiled and placed her head on his chest. Sam held her close, caressing her.

"I thought I lost you." Abigail whispered.

"I would never leave you. It would take a whole army to drag me away from you." Sam replied.

The two stared at each other and the longer they stared the more they realized that they couldn't live without one another. They came together with a fiery passion. Both of them moaned as their lips met for the first time. Their kiss was emotional and sensual. Sam held Abigail tightly as he expressed how he truly felt about her.

"Oh, Sam…" Abigail muttered as his lips left her mouth and traveled south. He grabbed the back of her neck and sucked on her skin. He licked her neck and then kissed her lips once more.

Electricity surged through Abigail as the hairs on her arm stood up from the excitement.

Buttons were unbuttoned, clothes were shed, and the two stood naked in the room. Sam groaned as he looked upon her nakedness once more. He noted her pale skin, her perky breasts and her brown hairy wet mound. Each of her features made him hard as all the blood rushed to his cock.

Abigail was impressed by Sam's muscles. He was well defined, and he looked to be a descent of Hercules himself. His dark skin and ridged core made her thighs quiver. Abigail's eyes drifted towards his enlarged member. She'd never seen a man so big before. She trembled at his size and her heartbeat tripled its pace.

"Like a moth to the flame, I am captured by your beauty. From the first time I saw you, I knew you were different." He complimented.

"Different how?" She asked.

"You were the only woman who took my breath away."

"Oh, Sam," Abigail moaned as she kissed him once more. Sam's hands rested on her hips as their tongues met in an erotic embrace. Their mouths seemed to be stuck together as they made love. Sam's hand gently slid down her smooth pale hip to her wetness and he placed a finger between her thighs. Abigail moaned softly as he wiggled it inside her. The quicker he moved the louder she became. She placed her head in the nook of his neck as the pleasure took hold of her. She gasped for air as her climax crept near.

Sam removed his finger and Abigail felt like begging for him to slip it back in. She was nearly there, instead she was treated to something better.

They fell back into the bed and Sam laid on top of her, as he spread her legs with his hand, he rubbed his length a few times before entering her. Abigail gasped as his thickness stretched her out. She never felt a man like Sam before. She held his back tightly as he pumped in and out of her rapidly.

Grunting, Sam held Abigail's ass as he made love to her. He never felt a woman like Abigail. He loved how soft her skin was and how she moaned his name. His hands drifted towards her legs and spread them wider allowing for deeper penetration.

"Oh, Sam. That feels good."

"You like that?"

"Yes, take me. Please take me." Abigail begged, before Sam quickened his pace. He moved at a hastened pace, pounding into her, using every ounce of energy he had. Abigail held on to his body as wave after wave of pleasure crashed into her. She closed her eyes as she felt that spark once more. She felt it in her stomach first, this fluttering feeling until it rose and exploded.

Her orgasm swept her up, knocking the air out of her lungs. The room seemed to spin as she was taken out this world. She could barely think or speak from the action. Sam's lips crashed into hers once more as he kissed her. He sucked on her lip as he continued to bury himself into her.

"Sam…"

"Yes, baby." He muttered as his face was buried into her neck.

"Hold me tight and never let go."

"I will. I always will." Sam held her back as he continued. Abigail wrapped her legs around his torso and then rolled with him in bed so she could be on top.

Sam laid on his back looking up at the goddess who was servicing him. His hands rested on her hips as he watched her ride him. His hands then drifted higher to her breasts where he massaged and kneaded them. His thumb stroked her pink nipple and Abigail giggled from his touch.

"You certainly like my breasts."

"I do. I love the way my dark hands blend with your pale skin. It's a beautiful sight. Almost like looking into a sunset. When I see this, I know that God is real, and he created you just for me."

"As he did for me." Abigail replied as she leaned forward and kissed Sam. As he kissed her, he held her butt, pounding her from the bottom. Abigail let out another moan as once more she felt that magical feeling return.

Sam shifted his weight and ended back on top again. He held her legs, grunting as he pumped in and out of her. Looking down he couldn't help but to smile at the woman who'd stolen his heart. He never felt this way about someone before. He cared for her. Wanted to be with her. Not only was she beautiful and kind, she'd connected with him on many levels he never even realized he had. She was his and he never wanted to change that fact.

Lying there and looking up at the man who saved her life, Abigail felt something she never felt before. She felt connected to this man. Unlike her deceased husband, this man cared for her, he provided for her. He made love to her like no other. This man she laid with was different. She never thought she'd be with a negro man, yet she found herself wanting him.

Holding him tightly she came yet again. This second time was more powerful than the first as she moaned. She closed her eyes experiencing the pinnacle of pleasure.

Sam groaned and he too felt his climax fast approaching. He held her tightly and moaned as he released his seed inside her. When he was through, he remained inside her and pushed back a strand of her hair.

"I love you," he muttered.

Abigail's eyes opened wide from his admission. A smile curved on her face as she looked back at him. She never admitted this to a man before, but with Sam it felt right.

"I love you too," she replied.

"Will you marry me?" He asked.

Abigail laid there in shock as she looked back in his eyes.

"Really?"

"Yes, I told you that I didn't want to get married unless I felt something and right now, I feel like gravity doesn't exist with you. I have so many butterflies in my stomach that I feel like I must call the doctor."

"I feel the same way, Sam. I accept. Let's get married."

"Aww, baby. You just made me the happiest man on Earth." He leaned forward and kissed her once more. As they laid in bed together, they both talked about their future together as husband and wife. Giving their romantic coupling the happy ending it deserved.

Epilogue

Sam was nervous and he didn't know why. He's been in more gunfights than he cared to admit, but these next five minutes scared the life out of him. He stood at the altar waiting. Besides him was the pastor. Sitting in the pews were all the townsfolk of the outpost. In the front was Thomas as he was being held by Madame Eva.

Sam wore his best suit today. Not an inch of dirt or mud could be found. When the doors opened and Abigail walked down in her white dress, Sam, nearly fainted. Just when he thought he'd seen it all, Abigail managed to surprise him yet again. She was carrying a bouquet of freshly picked yellow flowers and she had a large smile on her face. When she arrived at the alter, she winked at Sam.

"Hi, you look handsome." She complimented.

"And you look more beautiful than a rose. Are you ready to become my bride?"

"I've been ready since the day you invited me into your house."

The two turned and faced the pastor as he performed the service. At the end he looked at Sam and asked, "Sam Wilson do you take Abigail as your wife?"

"I do." Sam replied.

"And Abigail McToole do you take Sam as your husband?"

"I do." Abigail grinned.

"By the power invested in me by God and the state of Kansas, I now pronounce you man and wife. Sam you may kiss your bride."

Sam grinned and dragged Abigail close. "I've been waiting for this for a long time."

"Me too," Abigail replied as she kissed Sam.

And from that moment on, the U.S Marshal and his bride lived happily ever after.

A Sneak Preview of A Debt Owed

Blurb

By a stroke of luck, James' life as a landowner and former slave is just beginning - little does he know he is granted the love of his life as well.

Born in the eighteenth century, James Freeman is a black slave and an honorable man. When James saves a British General, Edward Byron, during the American Revolution, he is forever indebted to him - granting James new opportunities as a free man.

Victoria Byron is the most beautiful in the county and the most eligible debutante of the season thanks to her wealthy father, the Duke of Greenville, Lord Bryon. In an unexpected turn of events her father promises her hand in marriage to a black slave and gifts him a large portion of land for his heroic acts in the war. Victoria is outraged and believes her prospects to be ruined. Her courtship to James turns out to be more promising than expected and their chemistry is undeniable.

Will James and Victoria have the happily ever after they always dreamed of?

Preview

"Retreat! Retreat!" Lt. General Edward Byron shouted. The Duke of Greenville's face was covered in mud, sweat, and blood. The air around him didn't seem like it was enough as he took long-winded breaths. His bones felt brittle in the cold winter of South Carolina. It was January 17th, 1781, and his men were losing ground in Cowpen, South Carolina.

"Retreat!" He screamed once more over the bugle horn. After cutting down a colonial, he continued to wave the retreat with his sword. However, his attempts were futile. They were overrun. Dozens of rebels had already broken through their lines, and his men were scattered across the field. He knew his soldiers were either dead or close to it.

The Lt. General had been on the front lines for the past three years and nothing about the war was easy. During his time, he learned that the traitors to the crown were as tough as they come. They didn't give an inch and were willing to sacrifice everything for their cause. His troops were the opposite. They were tired, hungry, and missed home. It was hard to rally them for a cause they cared little for.

If you asked the Duke whom he was fighting, he would say for King and Country, however, in truth, he fought to stay alive to see his wife and daughters again. They were all he cared about in life.

"Come on lads, fall back!" Edward commanded. Another rebel charged with his bayonet and the Duke parried the blade out of the way before sticking the soldier with his sword. The battle was chaotic. Orders weren't being followed, mistakes with the vanguard were made, his men were scattered, not holding their positions. There was nothing left to do but retreat.

As they fell back to the tree line, the colonists were hot on their trail, firing at their backs, chasing them away. Edward tried to help his men as much as he could, but even he could tell it was every man for himself. He pushed his legs as fast as he could carry himself. As he ran, he reminded himself of his wife, Elizabeth, and his daughters Virginia and Victoria. He had to live for them. He had to stay alive.

He heard the snap and the pop of the bullets nearby. He attempted to duck for cover, but he was too late. Pain sprung to his shoulder, and he collapsed on the forest floor. Seconds later, he heard the patter of footsteps, and he turned to meet his foe. A group of ten militia all surrounded him, their bayonets at the ready.

Knowing it was the end, Edward lowered his head in shame and said, "I yield."

The largest of the ten spat tobacco and stepped forward. "Who are you?"

"I am Lt. General Byron. I am surrendering. I demand to speak to your commander to discuss terms."

"You're looking at him." He snarled.

"You're not wearing an officer's uniform."

The men laughed. "We're a bit different than you redcoats."

"As you wish. What are your terms?"

"There are no terms. As far as I am concerned, you're a redcoat, and all redcoats must die. Ain't that right, lads?"

Several of them nodded. Edward took a step back realizing that these men were not going to follow the standard rules of engagement. Just by looking at their eyes, Edward could see their evil intent.

"Where is your sense of honor? Are you not gentlemen?"

"Ha, gentlemen? This is war. Men die in war all the time. Any last words?"

"Please..." Edward begged. "I have a wife and children..."

"You should have thought about them before you crossed the sea. Fire on my mark! Aim!"

Edward closed his eyes, accepting the future pain, but before anything could happen, he heard a thunderous yell. Opening his eyes, he saw an African man with a pistol and hatchet in his arms. In a blink of an eye, he fired his gun, hitting the militia commander in the neck. He fell to his knees as he gurgled blood. Before the others had a chance to fire, this man was already on top of them, hacking and slashing through them like paper.

Edward watched with amazement as he took on nine men. He was the biggest man he ever saw, yet he moved like a rabbit, impossible to catch.

As the black man got rid of another soldier, his back was turned, and one rebel managed to load his musket. Before he could fire, Edward joined in the fray, sticking his blade in his backside. He assisted his savior taking out another two men.

When the last man had fallen, Edward kneeled. He was weak, as he had lost a lot of blood, and he could barely stand. Before he could fall to the ground, the black man grabbed him and helped him up.

"I got you, masta,"

"I'm not your master," Edward grunted.

"All white men are masta."

"Sadly, you are mistaken. What's your name?"

"James."

"Well, James, you saved my life. What were you doing out here?"

"Runnin.' Plantation not far. I ran from my masta to be free. You free me?"

Edward chuckled, realizing that he must have heard the king's proclamation saying that any slaves fighting for the British would earn their freedom.

"I can, but you must join our cause. However, seeing how you managed to kill seven men with just a pistol shot and hatchet, I can vouch for your fighting skills. Do you want to join us?"

"Yes."

"Good. My name is Lt. General Edward Byron; you may call me General or Duke Greenville, understood."

"Yes, masta."

"No," Edward shook his head and placed his hand on James' shoulder. "You are no longer a slave. You are a part of his majesty's army. You are a British soldier now. Understood?"

James nodded.

"Good, now help me walk." James stood beside Edward and placed Edward's arm over his shoulder and supported his weight. "Our forces should have retreated to the north side of the river, so that's where we must go. Do you know how to get there?"

"Yes, General."

"There you are. You are learning."

A small smile spread on James' face.

"Right then, off we go."

James nodded and carried Edward through the forest. Throughout their way, they continued to meet colonial forces, but through it all, James protected Edward, killing anyone that got in their way.

A day later, they regrouped with the rest of the battalion. After being treated by the medics, Edward found James resting at a tree away from the rest of the soldiers. He smiled at the gentle giant and secured the brown wrapped parcel underneath his arm. Before approaching, Edward stared at the brute. He wore a bloodstained tattered white tunic, brown trousers, and was shoeless, with rags wrapped around his feet. Edward was amazed that he had the willpower to walk through the forest without footwear.

"James?"

"Yes, General?"

"Thank you for saving me."

James nodded.

"I am forever in your debt. Those men would have killed me if you haven't come along."

James nodded once more.

"Do you know what debt means?"

James nodded again.

Edward laughed. "No, I don't think you do. It's okay, I'll explain it to you. A debt is an obligation to pay back a cost that is owed."

James narrowed his brow and Edward chuckled again. "Ah, yes, the English language is something of a mystery to you. I guess it makes sense, why teach a slave proper English when all you care about is their physical output. Don't worry about the definition, I'll teach you one day. You see James, I owe my life to you.

In return for my life, I am going to turn your life around. If we survive this war, I promise you, I'll make you an English gentleman, you'll learn how to read and write, how to speak proper English, and even own land."

"Land?"

"Yes, property. If I'm lucky I'll convince the King to make you a Baron in my county."

"Me, a Baron?" James asked, pointing to his chest.

"Yes, as crazy as it may seem, you would be one of the first African lords in England, but you save my life. I would be dead if it wasn't for you."

"Thank you, General."

"No, thank you."

A large smile spread across James' face.

"Ah, I almost forgot. If you are going to be a lord, you must start dressing like one." Edward then handed the parcel to James. He unwrapped this present and his eyes grew bigger than saucers as he stared at the British regular uniform.

"I didn't know your size. I took the largest garment from the quartermaster. How does it fit?"

James quickly disrobed from his rags and got dressed. His feet felt tight in the leather boots, but he'd never experienced so much warmth from clothes before.

"Shoes," James said, pointing at his feet.

Edward didn't need translation to know what James was referring to.

"A bit tight?" Edward asked.

James nodded.

"They'll stretch out. Is this your first-time wearing shoes?"

James nodded again. Edward laughed and placed his hand on James' shoulders. "I'm sure you'd be experiencing a lot of "firsts" from now on. Are you hungry?"

"Yes, General."

"Good, so am I. I heard one of our sharpshooters killed a deer. We should get a good meal tonight."

James smiled, "Thank you, General."

"I am in your debt, James. There will be many more acts of kindness from me. In fact, your first lesson starts tonight. I will teach you what debt is. Now, come on, I can smell that venison from here."

Continue to read more here:

https://www.amazon.com/gp/product/B09TTLPH1J/

About the Author

Remy Marie is an interracial romance author who loves to write about charming heroes and brave heroines. While writing never came naturally for Remy, he continued to strengthen his craft, by constantly reading and writing. If he is not writing or reading, he is usually watching TV with his supportive wife, loving his toddler, aggressively cheering for his college and professional sports teams, playing video games, or crunching numbers at his daytime job. If want to learn more, please go to the social media sites below.

https://twitter.com/remymarieauthor
https://instagram.com/remymarieauthor
https://remymarieromance.blogspot.com/
https://www.goodreads.com/user/show/72321338-remy-marie

I am on buymeacoffee.com too! Using this site helps me fund future projects! Each donation is used for editing, cover, and marketing costs! If you want to read more of my work, donating to my site will help me produce more books! Follow the link below to donate!

https://www.buymeacoffee.com/remymarieauthor

Works by Remy Marie

Short Stories

Eastcliff Romance University Series

Novellas

Novels

Jasmine Phillips has always had her sights set high, and it seems like she has everything figured out. She has the grades, the looks, the money—and let's not forget her perfect boyfriend. To anyone on the outside looking in, she has the perfect life. Little do they know, it's not what it seems. Despite her stellar grades and top percentile MCAT score, her parents still aren't happy. Jasmine's surgeon parents want her to follow in their footsteps while she wants to pursue a career in pediatrics. However, this turns out to be the least of her worries. Her perfect, med student boyfriend is determined to ruin her future along with his own. When he lays his hands on her for the first time, Jasmine's life is thrown into turmoil and Brock Givens seems to be the only one able to keep her life from spinning out of control.

Brock Givens might seem like an average dumb jock at a glance but to people who know him, he's much more that. While a football star, he's also smarter than most give him credit for and has a passion for more than just football, but that doesn't mean he's without issues of his own. Brock's troubled past and childhood trauma are impacting his football career and threatening his future. Jasmine tries to be there for Brock as a friend but they seem to be getting closer and closer each day while denying there is anything more than friendship until their mutual need for comfort and support brings them closer than they anticipate.

Content Warning, contains scenes of domestic abuse, sexual assault, and racism.

The Alpha Nanny

She needs money. He masks his pain. Life gives them a second chance, but reality may tear them apart.

Deena Zheng is in over her head. With her father's mounting medical bills, a townhome in disrepair, and more stress than one person should bear, she does all that she can do to stay afloat. Out of options and desperate to pull her family out of the red, she must get out of her comfort zone and accept a nanny position with her firm's notoriously impossible client or risk her family's livelihood.

Jesse Grant struggles to get past his grief after losing the love of his life. Ever since her death, the billionaire hedge fund manager has used alcohol to mask his pain and, in the process, lost a part of himself. With a young son to raise and a business to run, he must pull himself together before he jeopardizes everything he's worked so hard to build.

When they meet, the physical attraction is undeniable, but their personal demons and new professional relationship will make any hopes of pursuing a relationship too complicated for either to handle. Will they ignore their growing feelings for each other and keep their relationship strictly professional or will outside forces force them to reveal the truth?

Find out in this steamy second chance interracial AWBM contemporary romance!

https://www.amazon.com/dp/B07VRXCZHD

The Date Lottery

Victoria Evergreen has nothing going for her: she's a mere store clerk, reeling from the after-effects of a terrible breakup, and the only saving grace in her life is her best friend, Sherri. But when Tori chances upon a $10,000 lottery ticket to an invite-only date contest, her life takes an unexpected turn. Enter Dhruv Patel, Olympic skier, international lawyer, dream hunk. The two chance upon a beautiful, electrifying romance, but little does Dhruv know that Tori stole the lottery ticket. And little does Tori know... Dhruv holds secrets of his own. Will their respective secrets cost the couple their newfound love, or will they move past them and emerge stronger? Find out in this sizzling bwam romance.

https://www.amazon.com/dp/B07ZQV6LHC

Do you want to have updates on all things Remy Marie? Subscribe to my monthly newsletter!

http://eepurl.com/c6fynz

www.ingramcontent.com/pod-product-compliance
Lightning Source LLC
Chambersburg PA
CBHW061444160726

47995CB00003B/1026